...ndow!

Mom
April 15, 1990
Easter Day

Be sure to look for all the great McGee and Me!
books and videos at your favorite bookstore.

Focus on the Family
PRESENTS

A Star in the Breaking

Bill Myers and Ken C. Johnson

Tyndale House Publishers, Inc.
Wheaton, Illinois

For all the Fussles and Fusslettes

Front cover illustration copyright © 1989 by Morgan Weistling
Interior illustrations by Nathan Greene, copyright © 1989
 by Tyndale House Publishers, Inc.

Library of Congress Catalog Card Number 89-51393
ISBN 0-8423-4168-4
McGee and Me! is a trademark of Living Bibles International
Copyright © 1989 by Living Bibles International
Printed in the United States of America

1 2 3 4 5 6 7 8 9 95 94 93 92 91 90 89

Contents

When he [Jesus] noticed that all who came to the dinner were trying to sit near the head of the table, he gave them this advice: "If you are invited to a wedding feast, don't always head for the best seat. For if someone more respected than you shows up, the host will bring him over to where you are sitting and say, 'Let this man sit here instead.' And you, embarrassed, will have to take whatever seat is left at the foot of the table!

"Do this instead—start at the foot; and when your host sees you he will come and say, 'Friend, we have a better place than this for you!' Thus you will be honored in front of all the other guests. For everyone who tries to honor himself shall be humbled; and he who humbles himself shall be honored" (Luke 14:7-11, *The Living Bible*).

ONE
Beginnings . . .

The creature rose to his feet. His nostrils opened wide. The scent of his prey was still fresh. Silently he searched the dwelling for his next victim.

Mostly humans lived there. At times they could be a bother. Today they were of no concern to the creature. Today he sought a vile and smelly beast that had invaded his world once too often. "This loathsome thing must be taught a lesson," the monster reasoned. "And I will be its teacher!"

And a fearful teacher he was. . . .

His large, misshapen head was covered by reddish orange shafts of hair. On top there were two menacing gray horns. His mouth hung open and you could see a drooling tongue and sharp, jagged fangs.

But the most hideous feature was his eye—one huge, red, swollen eye in the middle of his forehead. It looked around, back and forth, searching for its victim, who was hiding somewhere among the humans.

Suddenly the eye caught sight of the victim. It was a short distance away, sound asleep! The poor, unsuspecting fool.

But, just to be safe, the monster froze in its tracks. Any sudden movement now might alert the animal. Then quietly, with the speed of a leopard, he moved forward. . . .

Unaware of the deadly stalking game going on in their living room, Nicholas and his two sisters watched TV. But not just any TV—this was "TRASH TV," The kids' game show where the contestants are slimed, gooped and, you guessed it, "trashed."

Right now one of the kids was having a dickens of a time trying to make it up the "Slime Slide." Each time he tried to crawl up the chocolate-covered slide his feet slipped out from under him and down he went in the goop.

Sometimes it was *plop*, sometimes *splat*, or even *slurrrrrrp*. Whatever sounds the kid made, they were no more disgusting than the way he looked. There were worse ways to go, though. After all, drowning in a vat of chocolate probably wasn't so bad. Besides, it sure looked funny. And Nicholas and Jamie sure were splitting a gut over it.

But not Sarah . . .

Sarah was above that sort of thing. Sure, she sat in the room with the other two. Sure, she heard everything that was going on. However, at the mature age of thirteen (almost fourteen) she really was quite beyond all that childishness. Instead, she sat curled up on the sofa, reading one of those Hollywood teen magazines. You know the type, with TV stars all over the cover and anti-zit advertisements all over the inside.

Little sister Jamie, on the other hand, was into the show. Normally she's kind of a shy kid. You know, real sensitive like. In fact, she probably takes everything way too seriously. But boy is she smart. I mean, if you're thinking of coming down with some kind of disease, try to hold off until she gets through medical school because she's the one who's going to find the cure.

Nick was having a good time, too. He never missed the show. And he was constantly amazed at how stupid and clumsy the contestants were. He could do better with his eyes closed. In fact, he'd even sent his name in as a contestant. If they'd just pick him, he'd show them. Of course, they'd never pick him. That sort of thing never happened to normal kids. That sort of thing never happened to average, run-of-the-mill people like Nicholas Martin. . . .

The fanged monster moved fast. He was in the kitchen. Quickly he closed in on his sleeping victim. The thrill of the chase raced through him, giving him even greater speed.

Suddenly, one of the humans stepped into his path. It was the older one. The Grandma. Probably fixing dinner.

With amazing agility the monster leaped to one side, narrowly missing a collision. Good thing, too. A collision would have alerted both his victim and the rest of the household.

11

Catching his breath, the courageous monster focused on his victim. He would have to move quickly now before anything could warn his prey. But "quickly" was his middle name. . . .

Back at the TV, the trashing continued. Only this time the other contestant was the victim. Again there was a lot of *squishing* and *squashing.* And again there was a lot of laughing and groaning by the studio audience.

"Oh no," the Host yelled. "I hope that doesn't taste as bad as it smells!"

More laughter.

Nicholas and Jamie could only look at each other.

"Yuck," Jamie said.

"Yuck," Nicholas replied.

Sarah, not to be outdone, finally raised her regal head. It only took her a moment to judge the situation. Then from her lips came the wisdom only a girl going on fourteen could have. It was a single word. The one word she used to describe almost everything in her life these days. She used it to describe all of her friend's actions. She used it to describe the clothes her mother picked out for her. She especially used it when she emptied the cat box.

"Gross," Sarah said. Then she turned the page in her magazine and went back to reading.

Obviously the girl didn't appreciate the finer details of being trashed. She didn't appreciate the oozing orange slime in the hair. She didn't appreciate the maple syrup running from the hands to the elbows and into the arm pits. She didn't even appreciate the classical and ever popular pie-in-the-face.

Luckily, Nick did.

Now only a few feet separated the creature from his victim. Opening his gigantic mouth, he stretched his hairy hands high above his terrible head. His approach had been silent and swift. Now, at last, the sleeping beast lay before him—an unsuspecting bag of fur.

The rumblings of a victory howl began low and deep in the monster's throat. It rose and built with unearthly volume until it exploded from his fanged face: "OOOOAAGGHHUBAGGAGABOOONNESSS!!"

(Translation: "I got you now, Fuzz Face!")

Although the monster had won numerous shriek and scream contests (he even had a degree in Screech Speech), he knew this scream was his best yet.

So did his victim. . . .

The poor animal jumped from his sleep like a flea on a hot rock. In fact he barely touched the ground as he leaped over my head and raced for protection from my monster mask.

Oh, uh, yeah, maybe I forgot to mention . . . it's just me . . . McGee. I'm the monster. Or rather, I'm the one wearing the monster fright mask. When I saw that furry freeloader, Whatever, the family pooch (or should I say, "mooch"), run like a rabbit, I nearly fell over laughing.

Now don't go feeling too sorry for the fuzz ball. He and I sorta have a running gag going between us. I play gags on him . . . and he just plain makes me gag! (I think I'm allergic to ugly.) Anyway, wearing a fright mask was fun. From the laughter going on in the family room I could tell the kids were having a good time, too.

I moved in for a closer look. . . .

Back on the tube, "Trash TV" had started to wind down. The two contestants stood together and tried to grin through the slime that kept sliding down their faces.

"Nice effort," the Host said. He reached out to shake the winner's hand. It was a boy. Then as the kid reached out to take the Host's hand, the Host yanked his away. "But keep it to yourself," he snapped.

The Host was that kind of guy. His name was Bill Banter. One minute you thought he liked kids. The next you weren't so sure. He was funny, though. Always had a wisecrack for everything. Sometimes, though, you weren't sure whether he was laughing with the kids or at them. In fact, sometimes you weren't sure whether he was a great guy or just a smart-aleck creep.

"Now," Banter continued, "for next week's contestants. Shena, do we have the cards?"

Some cheerleader-type kid raced up to him with a couple of cards.

Back in the living room Nicholas leaned forward. He'd seen this part of the show a billion times. A billion times he'd hoped they'd read his name, and a billion times they didn't. Still, he always listened carefully . . . just in case.

"All right . . . from the town of Ashcroft we have Amy Packard." Banter threw the card over his shoulder as if he didn't care. That was part of his image, not caring. "And from Eastfield . . . Nicholas Martin."

For a moment the living room was still. Had Nicholas heard right? Had the man said what he thought he'd said? Even Sarah looked up, a little startled.

Finally Jamie shouted, "That's you!"

Then the room exploded. Everyone started shouting and yelling at once.

"You won, Nicholas! You won!"

"I don't believe it!"

"Way to go!"

"I sent that card in months ago. . . ."

"All right!"

On and on they went, slapping Nick on the back and high fiving. Sarah even managed to lose her place in the magazine.

Bill Banter wasn't done. He was still holding the card with Nick's name on it and talking.

"Shhh, shhh," Nicholas said. "What's he saying? . . . listen up . . . shhh. . . ."

"Guys," Banter said, looking into the camera. "Can we get a close-up of this?"

The camera jerked and bounced into a close shot of the card.

"For those of you who think this show ain't art," Banter said, "one of the reasons we chose ol' Nicholas is this little drawing he included."

It was a drawing of McGee. But not just any old drawing: it was McGee as the mighty superhero

Major Mishap, his chest thrust out, his cape proudly blowing in the wind.

I guess I shouldn't have been too surprised at seeing myself on TV. I mean, fame was bound to be mine sooner or later. It wasn't even one of Nick's better drawings of me. Still, it was me. I have to admit I did look rather dashing in my pose. It's little wonder that the TV audience and Nick and his sisters were all going nuts. How could they resist?

I pulled off the fright mask I was still wearing. After all, Nick and I were on our way to stardom. Wearing a monster mask would only spoil my image as a Hollywood leading man.

In fact, I was sure the harsh light in the living

room might already be spoiling my complexion! So I whipped out the sunglasses to protect my baby-blues. Not for me, of course . . . for my fans.

"All right," the TV Host was saying, "that's our show for today. So, until next time, this is your Host, Bill Banter, saying to each and every one of you Trash Heads . . . Hey, make like a fly and buzz off!"

He gave a wheezy little laugh. The music started blaring. The Martin kids kept cheering. Everyone knew things in the house would change. Everyone knew things would never be the same.

They were right. But the changes weren't exactly what any of them thought they would be. . . .

TWO
Munching with the Martins

"McGee or not McGee? That is the question."

I delivered my lines with such emotion I held the audience breathless. There I was, high up on the stage, the lights shining down upon my golden mane (you know, my hair). With a flip of my jewel-lined cloak, I pranced about the stage, totally at ease. My flawless performance continued to spellbind the crowd.

It was the seventy-fifth annual Shakespeare Fest and Pancake Supper in Griddle Grease, Texas. An artistic delight for theater lovers and syrup slurpers alike.

I, McGee, of course, was its star—the golden boy of stage and screen. It was me they'd come to see! Winner of dozens of awards, including seven Oscars, six Emmys, five Grammys, four Tonys, and the Lifetime Achievement Award for the most unsuccessful appearances on a TV game show.

It was me, the matinee heartthrob of millions, who packed the aisles. It was me, an idol among screen idols, who filled this night with greatness. It was the pancakes, pork sausage, poached possum eggs, and peanut butter waffles that filled the audience's bellies. I mean, it was all you can eat for a buck eighty-five. Who could blame them for feeding their faces till they dropped?

Unfortunately, that's just what they did. It seemed the audience had all come down with a bad case of stomach cramps. (I'm sure it was the food. It couldn't have been my performance.) In any case, the people were leaving in droves. The massive crowd was cut down to a few thousand . . . uh, a few hundred . . . a few dozen . . . OK, OK, there were six left. But I wasn't related to any of them, and they were all still awake.

Unfazed by the course of events, I brought the final act to its searing climax. Then fate struck a final blow. I was consumed by my brilliant performance. I was caught offguard by the sudden gasp from the crowd. Was it something I'd said? I looked up. A falling sandbag was about to steal the scene. I made a valiant attempt to escape its blow—to no avail. The sandbag struck me squarely on the noggin (the head, that is). Next thing I knew, I was kissing the stage floor.

When I rose to my feet, I found myself back in reality. The "sandbag" wasn't a sandbag at all. It was a fork! For a moment I tried to pretend it was the instrument of some pancake-packing patron. But I really knew it belonged to my good buddy Nick. He had an uncanny way of bringing me out of my daydreams. This was no exception. (Although being clunked on the head with a fork seemed a bit heavy-handed.)

While we're talking about reality, I suppose I should admit I wasn't really in a theater. Actually, it was suppertime at the Martin household and we were in the kitchen. No stage. No crowd. My faithful audience was just the Martin clan gathered around the table for chow. And they didn't even know I was there.

They weren't exactly eating pancakes and possum eggs, either. It was close, though. Supper was really one of Grandma's homespun specialties: cauliflower and cabbage casserole smothered in onion gravy. With a side order of boiled beets!

Yummy yum! It really set my taste buds to dancing. I'm sure it did Nick's, too. Unfortunately I was limiting myself to a low-cal diet of Reese's Pieces and root beer floats. I mean, a guy's gotta be light on his feet if he's going to be on "Trash TV." Especially if he wants to avoid catching a case of slime-itis. Believe me, this was one contestant who wasn't about to come outta that show looking like a two-legged hot fudge sundae.

Ah, yes. "The Show." I was perched on top of Nick's backpack under his chair. I began to dream about the endless possibilities that lay ahead for Nick and me. . . .

This was our big chance for stardom. I pulled out a small hand mirror and brush. Movie contracts, billions of bucks, awards, fame, fast cars . . . and all the quarter-pound burgers you could eat. And maybe, just maybe, a summer home right smack in the center of the freeway! Yeah, that's the ticket! My mind was abuzz with the dreams only the beautiful people can dream.

Meanwhile, the dinner conversation at the table was buzzing with excitement. The whole Martin family was jabbering about "The Show." My buddy, Nick, was the center of all the attention.

"What are you going to wear?" Sarah asked as she poked around her plate looking for something resembling food.

"Forget the clothes," I shouted from below. "What's my share of the prize money?"

"Nothing," Nick called down to me. He was sneaking a forkful of beets into his napkin.

"Nothing?" Sarah exclaimed.

Just then the phone rang and Mrs. Mom rose to answer it.

"I don't think they'll let you do that on TV," Grandma offered. (She was right. I know the name of the show is "Trash TV," but I don't think contestants in their birthday suits is the kinda trash they had in mind!)

"If you win a phone, can I have it?" Sarah asked. Like all teenage girls, Sarah couldn't survive without a telephone. In fact, if Mom and Dad would let her, she'd probably have one surgically attached to her ear.

"Telephone?" Mr. Dad questioned. "What about a trip to Hawaii?" (I noticed he pronounced it "How-wa-yah," so I knew what was coming. . . .)

"Hawaii?" the kids exclaimed, mimicking his pronunciation.

"I'm fine," Mr. Dad answered. "How-wa-you?" He raised his eyebrows and did a Groucho Marx impression that would empty any decent theater.

The kids groaned (which sounded a lot like a

22

herd of lovesick camels). One thing about the kids. They know good humor when they hear it. And this definitely wasn't it.

Meanwhile Mrs. Mom was finishing her conversation on the telephone. "Eight-thirty will be fine. See you then." She hung up and came back to the table.

"Who was that?" Mr. Dad asked.

"The counseling center," Mrs. Mom beamed. "They looked at my resumé and want me to come in for an interview." She was obviously pretty pleased.

"Congratulations. That's great," the kids chimed in.

"I'll bet they'll be glad to get someone of your experience," Grandma added.

Mrs. Mom smiled back. Getting a job that would help out in the community was important to her—and counseling was right up her alley. "I hope so," she said.

All this news of Mrs. Mom's possible job had caused the conversation to change tracks. Seemed like everyone forgot about Nick, "Trash TV," and all those great prizes we were going to get. Everyone but me, that is.

Once again I began to dream about the glory and fame. Unfortunately I didn't see Whatever, that pesky pooch, round the corner. He was obviously hoping to find some tasty morsel that had dropped from the table. Then he spotted me—and decided he'd settle for . . . A McGEE BURGER!

He snapped to attention. Then the killer K-9 started toward me. When I saw him coming I knew I had to think and think fast. No way I wanted to become a feast for Fido!

Bracing myself for battle, I took my first position of defense (which just happens to look an awful lot like running away). I leaped from the backpack and dashed between the pooch's hairy little legs. I raced for the safety of my upstairs fortress (which looks a lot like Nick's drawing table). The mangy mutt turned sharply and was hot on my tail.

Keeping cool, I took my second position of defense: running even faster and screaming for help!

Luckily, I was fast enough to make it up the stairs and up onto the table. Otherwise I would have had to resort to my third position of defense . . . whimpering and begging for mercy.

THREE
School Daze

Jamie had always looked up to Nicholas. As far as she was concerned, he could do no wrong. Whenever she had questions, she'd come to him for help. Whenever she was in trouble, she knew he'd be there. Most of the time, it was good having an older brother. It gave her kind of a warm, secure feeling. Jamie loved it.

Of course there were other times. . . .

Like when they played "Spies" in the basement. Nicholas always got to be the enemy agent. She always had to be the good guy. One time he had her gagged and tied to some water pipes, just like on TV. Actually, the game was going pretty well. Nicholas pretended to steal some top secret microfilm (which looked a lot like one of Jamie's old beat-up class photos). Then Mom called down that lunch was ready and the game was over. At least, it was over for Nicholas. In a flash he was up the stairs, plopped down, and gobbling up his tomato soup and grilled cheese sandwich. Mom made great grilled cheese sandwiches.

When she asked where Jamie was, Nick said he guessed she wasn't hungry. That's honestly what he thought. After all, she heard the call for lunch just like he did.

The real reason Jamie wasn't there didn't dawn on him until almost an hour later. Jamie wasn't coming out of the basement because she *couldn't* come out of the basement. Jamie was still tied to the water pipes!

All things considered, though, Jamie still loved her older brother.

Her older brother loved her, too. 'Course, he didn't come right out and say so. In fact, he did a pretty good job of disguising it when "the guys" were around. Still, Jamie always knew that when the chips were down, Nick would be there.

Today was one of those times. Or so she thought. . . .

Jamie and Nicholas entered the school and headed down the hall together—Jamie toward second grade, Nicholas toward fifth. Sarah was the only one who went to a different school. But that was OK. Sarah was the one who was different.

It had been over a year since Sarah had entered that strange and uncharted territory of "teenager-hood." It had been over a year since she'd decided she was too mature and grown-up to be seen with the "children." So now it was Jamie and Nicholas, the two "children," who stuck together and helped each other out.

"Mrs. Snyder wants us to draw our favorite animal," Jamie said.

"Yeah, so . . . ?" Nicholas replied.

"So I can't draw a wombat. Will you help me?"

Nicholas threw her a glance. She was smart. There was no doubt about it. Sometimes he forgot how smart.

"What's a wombat?" he asked.

Jamie could only roll her eyes. How could a big brother who was so smart be so ignorant sometimes? Everybody knew a wombat was a . . . well, it was . . . you know, a wombat. And it looked like . . . well, it kinda looked like a wombat, too.

Before Jamie could put all of this into words they were interrupted.

"Hey, Nicholas, where's your limo?" It was Renee and a couple of her girlfriends.

Great, Jamie thought. As if her brother's mind wasn't mushy enough already. Now it's not that Nicholas was girl crazy or anything like that. It was just that lately it seemed he talked to them more and more. And the more he talked to them, the more brain-dead he became.

"Oh, uh, hi," he said. Not a great comeback and everyone knew it.

Jamie took a deep breath. *Here we go again,* she thought.

"Big stars need big cars," Renee joked. "You're a celebrity now."

For a moment Nicholas wasn't following what Renee meant. Then he remembered: the show! Ah yes, The Show. What did she call him? A celebrity? Well now, he really hadn't thought of it that way . . . but it was true. People did watch the show, so they probably did hear his name.

Maybe Renee was right. Maybe he was just a little bit of a celebrity. Not a big star, mind you. No, nothing like that. But at least somebody had heard his name . . . and was treating him a little differently.

"All I did is, you know, send in a card," Nicholas said. But Renee wasn't listening. She was already whisking him down the hall, her friends close behind. Nicholas was her pal, and today she wanted everybody to know it.

"This is all so excellent," she said. Then remembering her two other friends, she nodded toward them, "You know Janelle and Heather."

The girls smiled. Could it be? Yes, the second one, Heather . . . was she actually blushing a little? Why?

Then it hit him. Maybe it was because of the show! Maybe she had heard his name on TV. He glanced at her. She was still smiling . . . and still blushing. Did his fame really have that affect on people? Hmmmm. He didn't know for sure. He did know one thing, though. If it was true, this was going to be one great week.

So down the hall they went. . . .

Renee chattering away.

Heather blushing.

Nicholas basking in what he hoped was a new-found popularity.

As for Jamie—Jamie, whom Nicholas always looked out for, whom he was so close to, who so desperately needed his help to draw the wombat . . .

She stood in the hallway. Alone. Completely forgotten.

Things were even better for Nick in class. For some reason Mrs. Harmon was late. While they waited for her to show, more and more kids started to gather around Nick's desk. Along with Renee, Janelle, and (of course) Heather.

It was great. Nick could do no wrong. Everything he said was clever. Every wisecrack he made brought laughter. I mean, if this was the price of fame, he wouldn't mind paying that bill for a long, long time.

"Con-grat-u-lations, Mr. Hollywood." It was Louis. He flashed his biggest grin, his white teeth gleaming out against his dark face, and sauntered up to Nick in his usual "everything's cool" style. The two of them had been good buddies ever since the time Nicholas had gotten trapped in Mr. Ravenhill's house (which everyone had thought was the scariest house in the world . . . but that's another story).

"So, where's the shades?" Louis asked.

"Shades?" Nicholas quipped. "Why would I want to hide a face like this with shades?"

Everyone laughed. He was on a roll and he knew it.

If there was one thing Louis could do, though, it was talk. "You're right," he grinned. "Better get him a paper bag."

More laughter. Maybe a little more than over Nicholas's joke. That was OK. Louis was a friend. Nick could share his popularity with a friend. As long as it didn't get out of hand.

Suddenly the classroom door flew open. There stood Coach Slayter, as menacing as ever.

"All right you jokers," he bellowed. "Sit!"

Sit they did. It was as though they were suddenly sucked into their seats.

Power. Coach Slayter loved it.

He stood at the door with a trace of a sneer across his face. It was meant to be a smile. But after twenty years of working with kids, a sneer was the best he could do.

He lumbered toward the desk—his barrel chest and belly swaying as he walked. It all used to be muscle. Back in the good old days—back in the Marine Corps when he terrified the new soldiers at boot camp. When he shouted into their faces and made them quiver like Jell-O. All that was behind him, though. Now, all he had to terrify were the kids at school.

"All right, listen up!"

The kids glanced at one another nervously.

"Mrs. Harmon is sick . . . or somethin'. I'm here as her replacement." He broke into his version of a grin again. "For the *whole* day."

No one groaned. No one dared. At least not on the outside. But on the inside everyone was thinking the same thing: *Why wasn't I lucky enough to come down with the flu? Or the mumps? Or, Why didn't I step in front of the bus this morning?*

Coach carried a soccer ball under his arm. He always carried some sort of ball. It was his trademark. And he never dressed up. Never. He always wore jogging outfits. Well, not really outfits—more like outfit . . . the same one every day. By the end of the week it always had a distinctive odor about it. "Eau de Gym Locker," everyone called it. We'd heard there was no Mrs. Coach on the scene. By the end of the week, everyone could understand why.

"Get out a clean sheet of paper," he barked. "Spelling quiz this morning."

This time a few groans did escape. But that was OK with Coach. At least he knew they were suffering.

As Nicholas reached into his desk for a piece of paper, he caught Heather glancing over her shoulder at him.

She smiled.

He smiled.

Hmmm, things were getting interesting.

"All right, first word . . . alememanen." He was reading off a sheet of paper. By the way he butchered the word it was pretty obvious he didn't know what he was reading.

He tried again. "Alemmemmanen."

Nicholas glanced up.

A couple of the kids snickered.

What was he trying to say? Was it *aluminum*?

The coach was turning a little pink in the ears. He cleared his throat and tried again. "Alemum . . . alemuma . . ."

More laughter.

"OK, I'll tell you what," he said as he closed the book. "We'll do this a little later. Right now, uh . . ." He was searching the desk for something—anything. Then he spotted it. "Get out your Health Fitness Workbooks and, uh . . . ." He madly flipped through the pages. He had to let them know he was in control. "Take a look at page, uh, chapter, uh . . . chapter four."

The kids exchanged glances. It was going to be a strange day. A very strange, long day . . .

And long it was. But by the time 2:30 rolled around the coach had finally found something he was an expert at. . . .

"So we had on a draw play up the middle. As soon as I see the linebacker shoot the gap, I spring to the outside!" The coach was so excited he was practically shouting. "Now, you're thinking, where's the free safety, right?"

Of course the kids were doing anything *but* thinking *Where's the free safety?* Some slept. Others stared at the ceiling counting the little holes in the tile. And Nicholas explored the various designs that could be made from wadded up paper and eraser rubbings.

"Well, they're coming on a blitz!" Coach was lost in memories. He could practically hear the crowd cheering. "So I'm heading upfield with a straight shot right for the goal. Suddenly—"

A sharp knock at the door startled everyone—including Coach. Mr. Oliver, the assistant principal, poked his head in the doorway. "Gus?"

Coach Slayter ("Gus" to his friends) was yanked out of his memories and suddenly found himself back in the classroom. No more cheering crowds. No more adoring cheerleaders. No more glory.

"Oh . . . Mr. Oliver," Coach said nervously.

"I didn't mean to interrupt."

"No, uh, please," Coach insisted. He edged closer to the desk, worried about how much Mr. Oliver had heard.

But Mr. Oliver paid no attention to the coach. Instead, he began to search the classroom, looking for someone. "I was just . . . ," he started to say, then he spotted Nicholas. "There you are."

Nicholas froze. What had he done wrong? He was sure he hadn't done anything . . . at least not that he knew of.

"I just wanted to congratulate you, Nicholas," the man said, breaking into a grin, "and let you know how proud we are of you."

Weak with relief, Nick smiled back. He wasn't sure what Mr. Oliver was grinning about, but he figured it wouldn't hurt to grin in return.

"You can be sure that, come this Saturday," Mr. Oliver said, giving him a wink, "we'll all be rooting for you."

Nicholas beamed. Ah, yes, The Show. Word *had* gotten around . . . more than he had dreamed. Even the bigwigs in the office knew. He was a celebrity now—an official celebrity. There was no doubt about it.

The bell rang then. As the kids gathered around Nick's desk, he realized something wonderful: This was just the beginning. He would rise to the top. He would make his school proud, his city proud— maybe even the whole state. He knew that some- day soon the name "Nicholas Martin" would be on everyone's lips.

And actually, it was true. His name *would* be on everyone's lips.

Though not exactly the way he hoped . . .

FOUR
A Night in Hollyweird

Nicholas was a good guy. Everyone who knew him liked him. Maybe it was because he never tried to be too cool. Or maybe because he always treated people the way he wanted to be treated (even if they didn't always deserve it). That was probably it—he treated people like he wanted to be treated.

He wasn't sure where he'd learned that. Probably from his folks. Or from the Bible. Or maybe both. You see, following God was important to Nick. Oh, he didn't make a big deal out of it. It was just that his friendship with Jesus was one of the most important things in his life. He loved God and God loved him. Plain and simple.

And because of that love Nick didn't have to go around trying to be something he wasn't. He didn't have to go around trying to be super-cool. (Cool, maybe, but not super-cool.) He didn't have to go around putting others down so he looked good. He didn't even have to go around making sure things went his way. Why should he? God loved him. God was his friend. God would take care of him. I mean, what are friends for?

Still, sometimes Nicholas forgot. Sometimes he'd get so carried away with something that he forgot God was in charge. He didn't do it on purpose. It just sort of happened. And with all the excitement about The Show, and all the attention he was starting to get, well, it looked like this just might be one of those times. . . .

"Nicholas, if you don't turn that light off in ten seconds you'll be grounded for life!" It was Mom calling from the bottom of the stairs. This was only about the zillionth time she'd told him. He had been so busy sketching and daydreaming that he didn't hear her.

He heard her this time, though. It probably had something to do with the "grounded for life" bit.

"All right, all right," he grumbled. With that he tossed the sketch pad onto his night table. He scooted down under the covers and dug out his radio microphone. He whistled quietly into it and immediately the light over his dresser went out. He whistled again, a lower note this time. The light over his drawing table went out. One last whistle, a higher one, turned off the lamp on his nightstand.

Besides sketching, Nick also liked to invent.

It seemed every week he invented something different. This invention, his famous "Whistle Activated Light Turner-Off-er," was one of his favorites.

To be a good inventor you also had to be a good

dreamer—and dreaming was something Nick did best. You name it and he could dream about it. Being on The Show was no exception. What would life be like now that he was almost a star? What would he do with all the money he won? All the fame? All the glory?

He had dreamed about it all through dinner. He had dreamed about it all through his homework. Now he would dream about it all through the night.

Yes-siree, tonight is the night. At last Nick and I are on our way to the famous Grutman's Chinese Theater in beautiful downtown Hollyweird. We're going to have our handprints captured forever in cement. Then we will unveil our new film, Bat Boys Go Ape!

Now, some of you are probably wondering how a world premiere works. OK, so some of you probably don't care. But for you classier folks who do care, let me tell you how it goes.

A mob of adoring fans lines the street and the entrance to the glamorous theater. Giant spotlights scan the night sky. Among the crowd is the famous film critic Eugene Shallow. He's interviewing the celebrities who have come out to pay tribute to one of their own (that's me . . . oh, and Nick). Listen. . . .

"This is Eugene Shallow outside the world-famous Grutman's Chinese Theater. We're awaiting the arrival of the hottest new star ever to grace the silver screen. Among our fabulous array of celebrities is none other than one of Hollyweird's most explosive actors. In fact, he arrived tonight in

a Sherman tank—probably to promote his new movie, Rumbo X: The Next to the Last Final Chapter of the New Beginning!

"Look! He's coming this way! Excuse me, Mr. Rumbo! Mr. Rumbo! What are your thoughts on this grand occasion?"

"Uh . . . wo . . . yoow, hey, oh . . . yoooow, uh, Adriaaan!"

"Right. Well said, Mr. Rumbo. Hold on folks, here comes yet another international star. That wacky lacky from way down under . . . Alligator Andee. He's arriving in his Kangaroo Caddy. Mr. Andee, what do you folks from the outback say on a night like this?"

"G'day, Mate."

"Very interesting, but it's night."

"G'day, Mate."

"Oookay fine. You must be memorizing the lines of your next flick."

"G'day, Mate."

"All right already."

"G'day, Ma—"

"Look, beat it, will you!"

Suddenly the roar of the crowd alerts Eugene to the arrival of the evening's honored guest . . . me. Oh, right, and Nick, too, if you want to count him.

The front of our limo pulls into view. The band plays the fanfare: Ta-Da-Da-Da, Ta-Ta-Da.

The crowd screams hysterically. (And I haven't even told any jokes yet.)

Our extra long limo continues to pull up. Again the band plays for our entrance: Ta-Da-Da-Da, Ta-Ta-Da!

38

The crowd is beside itself (which is OK by me 'cause that means there's twice as many of them!).

Our limo keeps on coming. (We're talking serious stretch here.) Finally the band tries one last fanfare (minus a few trumpet players who passed out on the last blast): Ta-Ta-Da, Ta-To-Tweep!

At last, to the mighty roar of the crowd (and the great relief of the band) our limo finally comes to a halt.

Through the tinted glass window I can see the cameras flash like fireworks. The crowd pushes in for a closer peek at us, their idols.

Now because of my fame I've grown somewhat accustomed to this kind of attention. Nick, on the other hand, is a bundle of nerves. I guess it's stage fright. So I figure I'd better take the lead and help the kid with his first session of "Meet the Press."

It won't be too tough to protect Nick. After all, the press is out basically to see me. They want to get some juicy story for their gossip papers. Or to catch one of my brilliant smiles for the fan magazines. And of course my fans are going wild begging for a lock of my hair or clippings from my toenails. (Fans can be weird like that.) But that's the cost of fame.

I adjust my tux and give the kid a look of encouragement. Then we nod to each other and lower our sunglasses into place. (Those flashbulbs can be murder on unprotected eyes.)

It's now or never. I reach for the limo door. I steady myself for the mob of adoring fans that will shower me with praise. I swing the door open and flash the "little people" my best devil-may-care smile—a sure crowd pleaser.

*Like a mighty rush of wind comes the crowd's
ringing response . . . like a mighty rush of . . . wind
. . . comes . . . uh, ahem . . .*

*The place is as quiet as a library. No, even a
library has some lady saying, "Shhhhh!" all the
time. This place could pass for a silent movie!
What's wrong?*

*Suddenly it occurs to me: Bless their hearts,
they're speechless! Yeah, that's it. They just can't
take all of me in. They don't know how to respond
to me, here, live and in living color.*

Then I hear someone whisper, "Who's that?"

*"WHO'S THAT?" What are they talking about?
Has Nick got out of the limo behind me? I turn
around to take a look. No, not yet.*

*Suddenly I hear a hissing sound. Rats, I told the
driver to check the tires before we left. But wait!
The hissing isn't coming from the tires. It's coming
from the crowd! I don't understand. Don't they
recognize me?*

*I stand a little taller making sure to block their
view of Nick. After all, there is no reason for him to
experience this terrible mix-up. But when I block
him, they hiss even louder.*

*Finally Nick is able to push his way out. He must
be pretty shook up 'cause he starts waving and
blowing kisses to everyone . . . as if he thinks
they've come to see him! Poor, confused kid.*

*Then the crowd sees Nick, and the whole place
goes nuts! Photographers, security guards, and millions of screaming faces. I don't understand.*

*I turn to look at Nick. Already a large group of
photographers has surrounded him. What a bunch*

of goofs. I dash over and leap between their cameras and Nick. Otherwise they wouldn't have gotten me in the picture.

From another direction a different group of newspaper reporters clusters around us. This group is dumber than the last. They keep calling out to Nicholas, "Mr. Martin, Mr. Martin, over here. Give us a smile."

How 'bout a brain?! Again I have to leap up in front of Nick to make sure they get me in the shot. There's no telling how many jobs I'm saving tonight. Just imagine what their editors would do if they went back to their papers without pics of me . . . me, the premiere's star.

Each time they try to take a photo of Nick's face

I'm there with mine. I can tell that the picture boys are getting on ol' Nick's nerves, too, 'cause every time I have to jump in to save the shot, he frowns.

At last comes the big moment. Eugene Shallow steps to the mike and invites us forward, saying, "Now for the traditional handprints in the sidewalk."

We cross to the concrete and bend down on our hands and knees. I still have to stretch to get into the photos. Boy! Don't these guys realize that they're only getting Nick in the shot? What kind of fan mag can use that?

"Now, gentlemen," Shallow continues. "Will you place your hands in the wet cement? We want this evening to be remembered, just like all the other great moments in Hollyweird history."

This next part you're not gonna believe. . . .

Nick and I place our hands firmly in the cement and a lone photographer leans forward. Once again I have to stretch to get into the picture (though Nick did provide a nice background).

Then, all of a sudden, Nicholas's hand shoots up behind me. As near as I can tell he probably sees a lock of my hair out of place and is trying to smooth it. Or maybe he's just overcome with nerves. Or maybe he's put his tie on too tight!

In any case, his hand comes down so hard that my head goes straight down into the wet cement! You can imagine how hard it is to spring back up in time to join Nick in our final picture. Somehow I manage, though. A good thing, too, because it's for the cover of Vanity.

Boy, will I look great! (Even with all the cement

gunk on my face.) I just know the Hollyweird Hot Shots will be calling me tomorrow, begging me to star in their next flick.

Then, somewhere in the back of my mind, I have this feeling . . . This is too good to be true. Somewhere, in the back of my mind, I have this terrible feeling that this bigger-than-life premiere is just another one of Nicholas's bigger-than-life dreams. . . .

FIVE
Fanning the Fame

The following morning Nicholas was up bright and early. Now that he was a star, he had lots of important decisions to make. What conditioner should he put on his hair? How much of Dad's after-shave should he use (and exactly where should he use it)? And what color sweater would best bring out the sparkle in his eyes?

Then there was breakfast. Gotta watch those empty calories. Gotta keep that waist slim and trim for your fans. Being a public idol isn't as easy as you might think.

Of course the rest of the family went on like nothing had happened. Dad left for work. Jamie was upstairs getting dressed. Sarah was at the kitchen counter madly trying to finish her algebra.

Nick grinned. *You gotta hand it to them*, he thought. *They're doing a pretty good job of pretending everything is normal.* Actually, that was probably best for the family. You know, not to acknowledge that they had a superstar in their very midst. He smiled gently. Too bad they wouldn't be able to ignore his fame forever.

In just one day he had risen from "Nick the Nobody" to, as Mr. Oliver put it, "Nick-I-just-want-you-to-know-how-proud-we-are of-you." His fame was spreading like fire. Who knew what today would bring. Yesterday he'd brought his school's vice principal to his knees. Today, the world.

"Nicholas, you got your bed made?"

It was his mother. What a silly question to ask somebody as important as Nick. But he'd play along. "Sure, Mom."

"Are your clothes picked up?"

"Yes." He was careful to let his voice sound a little irritated. She had to know he wasn't going to play the game forever.

"Mom, you look great." It was Sarah. She still stood at the counter doing her algebra.

Nicholas glanced up from pouring his cereal. It was true, his mom did look good—if you could be bothered with that sort of thing.

"Thanks, Honey," she said to Sarah. "Interview day at the center."

He'd almost forgotten. This was her big day. The day to get that job she wanted so badly. But Nick had other things on his mind. More important things.

"Sarah," he asked, "could you get me the milk?"

Without thinking, Sarah reached for the milk on the counter. She brought it over to the table for him.

Nick's response? Not a thank you. Not even a nod of the head. Instead, "What about the sugar?"

A little frustrated, Sarah turned and headed

back to the counter for the sugar.

"OK, guys, I'm off," Mom said as she headed for the door. "Wish me luck."

They did and she disappeared out the door. Meanwhile, Sarah set the sugar on the table.

Nicholas's response? "You forgot my spoon."

Sarah glared down at him.

He looked up, waiting. After all, he had too many other things to think about. Being a star was tough business. He didn't have time to wait on himself. Other people would have to start carrying some of that load.

Sarah reached for the sugar.

How kind, he thought. *She's going to sugar my cereal for me. . . .*

Then she threw a handful of it in his face. "I am not your maid!" she sputtered. With that she turned, grabbed her books, and stormed out the door.

Nicholas was stunned. What had gone wrong? Didn't she know who he was? Didn't she know what a privilege it was to wait on him?

"Does this mean you're not getting me my spoon?" he asked.

There was no answer. She was already gone.

Nicholas sighed heavily and started to brush the sugar off his sweater. Obviously the poor, dear child was just overcome with jealousy. *That's OK,* he thought with a grin. *She'll get used to it. They'll all get used to it.*

Unfortunately, school wasn't that much different from home.

47

It started OK. Nicholas was just cruising down the hall toward class. Sure, he had his shirttail out and collar turned up like he'd seen on TV. Sure, he had his sweater tied around his neck like the college kids. But, hey, looking super-cool was part of his image now.

"Oh, Nicholas . . ." Renee appeared beside him.

"Good morning," he said as he continued to saunter on down the hall.

"Listen, do you think you can get me Bill Banter's autograph? The guy's so cool. I mean, he's really funny."

Nicholas stalled. "Well, I . . ."

Since Banter was the host of "Trash TV" Nick knew he could get the guy's autograph, no problem. But there was something so uncool about one star asking for another star's autograph.

Luckily, Louis showed up before he had to crush Renee's feelings.

"Hey, Nick. Me and some of the guys were thinking we should go down to the studio with you and, you know, check it out."

That idea sounded even better to Renee. "Yeah! That'd be so excellent. We could all—"

Nicholas knew he had to put a stop to this immediately. He'd heard of this type of thing happening. Once a person becomes rich and famous his friends always try to tag along. "I don't know, guys," he said.

Louis and Renee looked at him, surprised. "What do you mean?" Louis asked.

Nick raised his eyebrows slightly, trying to look super-cool and bored at the same time. "I mean,"

48

he said carelessly, "how's it going to make me look? You know, if I come dragging in with a bunch of kids and stuff?"

"Kids?" Louis's never-failing grin started to fail. "So what do you think you are?" Noticing Nick's collar he reached over and gave it a flick. "Mr. Chuck Berry, with your collar all turned up . . ."

Having no idea that Chuck Berry was a rock and roller, Renee tried to help. "You mean Chuck Norris?"

Louis could only look at her. She could be so dumb sometimes. Before he had a chance to point this out, Nicholas butted in.

"Hey, look, guys. I'm the one who got on the show, all right? Not you. Me. Now I'll see what I can do. Maybe if you're lucky—"

"Hey," Louis interrupted. "Don't do me any favors."

"Me, neither," Renee joined in.

Nicholas looked at them. There it was again . . . jealousy. Just like with Sarah. What was wrong with these people? Didn't they know how lucky they were to be in his company? Didn't they know how blessed they were to have his friendship?

By the look on their faces it was obvious they didn't. Nicholas gave a long sigh. Too bad. Still, if that was the way they wanted it, that was the way they'd have it.

"Have it your way," he said. With that, he turned and headed down the hall.

The kids could only stare after him. They were amazed. In just a few short days their friend had gone from "Nick the Nice Guy" to "Nick the Knucklehead." All because of one little TV show.

Louis and Renee shook their heads. One little
show had filled their friend with so much pride
they couldn't stand being around him. If that's
what fame did to people, they didn't want anything to do with it—or with Nicholas. . . .

Meanwhile, Mom had been having her own battle
with pride. Before the family had moved in with
Grandma, before they had moved into the city,
Mom had taught at a small junior college. She
also worked as a part-time counselor.

So when the counseling center called her about
a job, she was excited. Counseling was something
she was really good at. When she went in for the
job interview she expected them to offer her something really "juicy." Unfortunately, "juicy" wasn't
exactly what they had in mind. . . .

"Mrs. Martin," they said. "We've looked over
your resumé. Your training and experience are
quite impressive."

She felt the pride start to well up inside. Of
course these people were impressed. With all her
experience they *should* be impressed.

"Unfortunately, right now," they continued, "we
just need someone to answer our telephones."

Mom couldn't believe her ears.

"We know that's not much of an offer to someone of your experience—but we really need the
help. Would you mind considering it? At least for
the time being?"

Mom forced a smile. She didn't know what to
do. She didn't know what to say. After another

moment she quietly stood up. She said she'd think about it. She shook their hands. Then she calmly left their office, got inside her car . . . and exploded!

How dare they! Don't they know who I am? What about all my training . . . my experience?! HOW DARE THEY!! Her insides were screaming all the way home.

Later, after dinner, after she had cooled down some, she heard another voice. It was also from inside—but this voice was much different. It was asking a different kind of question. . . .

"What would God want me to do? Sure, answering phones would be humbling. Sure, it seems beneath me. But they said they really needed someone to help. Maybe God wants me to be that someone."

"What? Are you crazy?" It was the first voice again—the angry one. "Serving God is one thing. But not as someone who answers telephones!"

"But . . . if I've really given him my life, if I really want to serve him . . . does it matter *how* I serve?"

"You're better than that! You're better than someone who just answers telephones!"

As soon as she heard that, she knew what the other voice was. She knew where it was coming from. She knew it was pride . . . her pride.

Here she was thinking she was hot stuff—that she was better than somebody else, than "someone who *just* answers telephones." As she thought about it, several Bible verses came to her mind. Verses that reminded her that we're not to think that way. Verses that reminded her that we are to consider other people as important as we are.

Mom sighed and sat down. Just for a moment, she'd forgotten that part of being a Christian means we're to put other people first. It means we're to treat others like they're as important—or even more important—than ourselves. It means looking for ways we can help and serve them.

She knew that when she stopped thinking the Bible's way—when she started thinking she was better than someone else—Well, there's only one word for it: Pride.

Still, though Mom knew it was pride, and though she knew it was wrong . . . it didn't go away. It stayed there in her mind. It kept arguing with her. It kept telling her that she deserved better.

So there she was . . . knowing what the Bible said, but also knowing what she felt. What should she do? It was like a war going on inside her head. Back and forth. Back and forth. And, at the moment, she wasn't sure which side would win.

That evening, up in his bedroom, Nick was also fighting with pride. He didn't *know* that was its name . . . not yet. He just knew that "being better than everyone else" wasn't as much fun as he thought. He was starting to lose his friends. And he was starting to feel very alone.

It was one thing for Sarah to turn on him at breakfast. That was expected. She was his sister. But to have his friends turn on him, too—that was a little tough for anybody to take. What was wrong with these people, anyway? What was their problem?

Of course, it never dawned on Nick that the problem might be his . . . that he'd let his pride convince him he was better than everyone else.

All he knew was that it was starting to hurt.

Oh well, at least he had McGee. . . .

SIX
Another Friend Bites the Dust

On the eve of the big show I was busy with some glamorous activities . . . I was pressing my pants. Hey, the way I look at it, it's not what you do so much as how you do it. I've got my own style of pant pressing. (But unless you kiddies at home are old enough to order a pizza over the phone without asking permission, leave this chore to your folks.)

First, you make sure you're wearing your best boxer shorts. A guy can look real goofy standing at an ironing board if he's wearing just any old pair of boxers. Me, I like a snazzy design on mine—you know, like little saxophones.

Secondly, make sure your shirt and tie are buttoned up nice and tidy. That way, if you forget to put on your pants they'll still let you eat in a fancy restaurant. (As long as you stay seated.)

Now it's time to get down to the actual job of pant pressing. I like to begin with the left leg first. Don't ask me why. I just feel the left side of things gets overlooked a lot. I mean, have you ever noticed people always say things like, "Oh, I'll just take whatever's left." Or, "Gee, nobody's home, I guess they left." Then there's the ultimate, "Oh, look . . . nothing's left!"

It hardly seems fair. So I just have a private campaign to keep a left outlook on life. (I know what you're thinking . . . "He's right.")

Anyway, after the left pant leg has been cared for, I usually check the iron to make sure it's not too hot.

I moisten my thumb (uh, you know, I give it a lick), then I lightly touch the iron. If the iron is too hot my thumb will make a sizzling sound—something like bacon frying in a skillet. If that's the case, I'll drop the iron and scream loud enough to give my tongue a charley horse.

On the other hand, if the iron is an OK temperature, I'll hold it up a second longer and check my reflection (just to make sure my hair is in place).

It was during this ritual that a shadow of doubt crossed my mind. We were going to be on TV, right? The whole world would see me, right? So, although I'm usually a classy dresser, I decided it wouldn't hurt to get a second opinion.

"Hey, Nick. What do you think about these pants with my checkered tie?"

Now Nick is not exactly what you call a "slave to fashion." You know, he doesn't always have to wear the latest styles in the latest colors. On the other hand, I never saw him stick his hair in orange dye or wear floppy red clown shoes. So I expected a fairly decent answer. So much for great expectations.

"Who cares?" he muttered with a shrug, barely

looking up from his homework.

"WHO CARES?" I protested. "I'm not going on that TV show in front of all my fans without looking my best!"

"'Your' fans got nothing to worry about, Mop-Top," Nick said, still not looking up. "You're not going on the show; I am."

I immediately saw red. I also saw Nick calmly turning the page of his textbook. What a perfect target . . . so I did the only sensible thing: I threw a spitwad together and let it fly!

"Oow!" he yelped.

A direct hit. Now for the verbal attack. . . .

"Listen, Sasquatch," I yelled. "You wouldn't be on that show if it wasn't for me . . . you jar head!"

Nick grabbed a scrap of paper, wadded it into a ball, and let me have it with one of his better comebacks: "Oh . . . oh, yeah?" he stammered, as he threw the paper.

Like I always say, Nick's about as clever as a tree stump when it comes to snappy replies. But when it comes to marksmanship (you know, having terrific aim), he's no slouch. The paper wad beaned me right on the noggin.

"Ferret Nose!" he blurted.

Hmmmm . . . Ferret Nose. Not bad. That's raising the stakes.

Whipping up a nearby walnut, I quickly placed it between two pencils and a rubber band and . . . ZING!

"Mutant Brain!" I bellowed, but the lucky little stiff deflected my shot with his notebook. This is war!!

Meanwhile, downstairs, little Jamie worked on her art project. Try as she might, she just couldn't get the wombat to look like a wombat. It had taken her two hours and ten pieces of paper—but the closest she got was something that looked part wart hog and part giraffe.

The girl definitely needed some help.

She glanced up the stairs. She knew Nicholas was busy. After all, he was a big star now. And besides, The Show was tomorrow. He wouldn't have time for little people like her. She bit her lip. Maybe if she went up and asked real politely— maybe he'd give her a hand . . . for old time's sake.

She decided to gather her things and give it a try. She looked up the stairs, took a deep breath, and started forward.

The battle was in full swing. Nick had on his Rams football helmet. He had also scooped up every eraser he could grab from his art table. Now, from his safe position behind the bed, he hurled them at me like cannon balls.

I, on the other hand, never cared for ground battles. I preferred an aerial assault. And I'm not talking Sopwith Camel, either. (Those are for beagles.) This baby was a top-of-the-line, two-tone, baby-blue jobber with a spitwad flinger mounted on each wing.

I banked left and brought my plane in, her guns ablazin'. . . .

Bop-bop-bop-bop-bop-boingggg!

Got him!

Nick cringed and grabbed a pillow to shield himself.

"Take that, Army Dog!" I cried as I brought my

bomber around for another attack. We airmen always hurl neat insults like that at our targets. It really shakes them up. Then, just for good measure, we throw in a crazy laugh: "MOO-MOO-MOO-HOOO-HOO-HAHAHAHA!!!!"

Desperately trying to regain his senses, my opponent hurled another Pink Pearl eraser bomb. "You missed me, Pickle Lips!" I heard him scream over the roar of my engines.

It was a lie. I got him fair and square. But for good measure, and to make him eat his words, I swooped down for another attack. . . .

Jamie was at the top of the stairs now—not far from Nick's room. Then she stopped, frowning slightly. What was that she heard? It sounded just like one of those old World War II movies. *That's pretty strange,* she thought. *Nicholas doesn't have a TV in his room.*

Puzzled, she started toward the door.

The smoke from the bomb bursts was so thick it was all I could do to keep from slamming my plane into a wall. The only way I could locate Nick was when he hurled another insult. "You'll never take me alive, Nose Hair!!"

What an imagination. I wasn't planning to take the fathead alive!

I took one last look at my bomb payload and checked the ammo rounds. One final pass around the room, dropping everything I had left, would put the whole place up in smoke. If I wasn't going on that show, no one was.

I tossed in another crazed laugh:
"Moo-Ho-Ho-Ha-Ha-Hah!!"
Then I dumped my payload. Every corner of the room exploded with bomb bursts and the rocket's red glare.
KA-BOOM!!!

Jamie was right outside Nick's room now. The noise was incredible—she could hear *booms*, *bangs*, and *rat-a-tat-tats*. She paused a moment. Should she open the door?

For the past couple years things had not exactly been what you'd call "normal." A lot of it started about the time Nicholas first created his cartoon buddy, McGee. Jamie knew that McGee was just a drawing, that he was just a make-believe character Nicholas sketched on his drawing pad. Still . . .

Every once in a while it almost seemed McGee was alive.

Maybe it had something to do with Nicholas always carrying around his pad and drawing McGee in all kinds of adventures.

Or maybe it had something to do with the imaginary conversations Nick pretended to have with his "friend."

Then there were those other times. Times like this one. Times when Jamie could hear all sorts of strange sounds. Sometimes they came from Nick's room. Sometimes they came from the backseat of the car. Sometimes, they came from weird places—like backpacks and cereal boxes!

Sure, Nicholas could just be making those

noises himself. After all, he had a pretty good imagination. Still . . .

Jamie had tried a number of times to catch
him—McGee, that is—*if* he was alive. But she'd
never been able to. It had always turned out to be
just Nicholas and his imagination.

Maybe this time would be different.

She reached out and put her hand on the door
knob. She turned it. Then with a deep breath she
threw it open and discovered . . .

Nothing.

No guns, no bombs, no smoke.

Nothing. Oh, there were some erasers on the
floor and some wadded up pieces of paper. But
nothing else. Not even Nicholas.

"Nicholas?"

Suddenly he popped his head up from behind
the bed. He looked kind of funny—all crouched
down with his Rams football helmet a little
crooked, like he'd just ducked real fast.

"What!?" He was startled.

"What . . . ," she glanced nervously about.
"What are you doing?"

"Nothing." He also looked kind of embarrassed.
He was always embarrassed when people caught
him with McGee. Now he figured he'd better make
an excuse about why he was on his knees behind
the bed. "I, uh, I dropped something. What do you
want?"

"I was wondering . . ." She cleared her throat. "I
was wondering if you could help me with my wombat drawing?"

Nicholas let out a sigh of frustration. Here he

was in the middle of World War III, defending the entire free world, and she wanted him to stop and draw a wombat?? Come on!!

"Jamie, I don't have time for that kind of stuff! Tomorrow's the big show. I gotta get ready."

She glanced around. It didn't exactly look like he was "getting ready." She started to point this out, but he cut her off.

"Besides, what kind of a dumb choice is a wombat, anyway?" No sooner had he said the words then he wished he hadn't. The look in his sister's eyes told him clearly that he'd hurt her feelings—badly. He tried to take it back, to make it better. "Listen, uh, if I have time, I'll do it when I get home."

It was too late. He could tell he'd already cut her. Maybe not with a knife—but sometimes his tongue and his words were even sharper than a knife. He hadn't meant to hurt her. It had just happened. It seemed a lot of things were "just happening" lately.

Of course, Jamie tried to be brave and pretend everything was OK. "Sure . . . thanks," she said. But as she turned and left the room, Nick could tell she was pretty close to crying.

He watched as the door quietly shut behind her. He wished he hadn't been such a jerk. But before he could decide what to do . . .

Splat-too-weeee!

. . . another spitwad.

"McGee! Just leave me alone!" Nick shouted angrily. Then he looked around. The little critter was nowhere to be found. "You're not going on the show and that's final!" Nick said, even more angrily.

No answer.

"McGee?"

Still no answer.

"McGee?" This time Nicholas called more softly.

He looked around again. Where was McGee?
Where'd he go? Finally, he spotted him—he was
back on a page in the sketch pad. His arms were
folded. His back was toward Nick. And he was no
longer alive. He had returned to just being a drawing.

"All right, fine," Nicholas said. "You want to be
that way?" The boy reached for the sketch pad
and slammed it shut. "Be that way!"

With that he tossed the pad across the room
and onto the floor.

"Who needs a stupid cartoon, anyway?"

Nick was mad. There was no doubt about it. *He* was the star. *He* was the one going on the show. Nobody else. Just *him.* Renee, Louis, Jamie—even McGee—if they couldn't handle it, that was their tough luck.

The room was strangely quiet . . . and Nicholas felt strangely alone. He threw one last glance to the sketch pad.

It lay on the floor, silent and still.

Forget him. Forget them all. He didn't need them! He didn't need any of them! Not even McGee!

Nicholas lay down on the bed, his head swimming with anger, with hurt . . . and with pride.

Now he was alone. Completely alone.

Well, that was OK. Because tomorrow was The Show. And he'd show them. He'd show them all.

SEVEN
Final Good-byes

The clock clicked to 7:00 A.M. and the alarm went off.

This was no ordinary alarm. It wasn't one of your blaring buzzers—the type that barges into your sleep screaming, "I don't care how good this dream is, it's time to get up!" Nor was it one of those useless radio alarms. You know, the type you can sleep through if you really want to.

No, this was a one-of-a-kind, Nicholas Martin custom-designed alarm. So of course, it was different.

For starters there was the clown with the pinwheel. As soon as the radio clicked on, the pinwheel started to spin. It lifted ol' Bozo off the clock and into the air until he crashed into a black, supersonic spy plane,

. . . which shot across the room on a line until it hit a target on the opposite wall,

. . . which triggered a red boxing glove,

. . . which dropped and banged into a

homemade sign that began flashing ALERT!
ALERT! ALERT!

. . . which gave off the appropriate alarm sounds,
. . . which made sure Nick would wake up.

Simple, right?

Only this time it didn't work. Mainly because
Nick was already awake.

He'd been up for hours trying on one shirt after
another. Then, when he finally found the right
shirt, his pants were wrong. So he began the same
thing all over again with his pants. Now at last
he'd found the right combination. (He had to; he
was running out of clothes.)

He stood in front of the mirror and put the
finishing touches on his tie. Ah, yes, the tie—something he only wore to weddings (and the one
funeral he'd been to). It's not that he hated ties.
It's just that, well, he had this thing about breathing. He liked to do it. And ties, he figured, had this
thing about not wanting him to do it.

He gave the tie one final pull to make it nice and
tight. Nice and uncomfortable, too. But hey, he
had an image to keep up.

Finally his eyes wandered to a sketch of McGee
he had tacked on the wall. He was in his Major
Mishap costume—complete with flying cape and
fearless grin.

Nicholas felt his heart sink. He and Major
Mishap had been through so much. They had
solved some of the toughest crimes together. They
had arrested some of the baddest of bad guys. Now
there was no life to the Major. Now, he was just a
drawing on a piece of paper stuck to the wall.

Nick tried to look away. He did, but only for a second. Soon his eyes were back to the drawing. He could feel the start of something hard and aching in the back of his throat. The two of them had had so much fun together. Now . . .

He looked over his shoulder to the sketch pad. It was still lying on the floor where he had thrown it. It was still closed. And silent.

The lump in Nick's throat was growing. He tried to swallow it, but it stayed. He and McGee were best friends. Or, at least, they had been. Now . . .

Nick tried his best not to think about it. But he knew he was going to miss McGee. He was going to miss him a lot.

He turned back to the mirror and checked himself out one last time. Satisfied, he crossed to the door. It felt strange not to have that sketch pad under his arm. He'd never been anywhere without it. Still, he wasn't going to beg McGee to come—no way.

Nick grabbed his coat and stopped at the door. He wanted to look back one last time. He wanted to see McGee standing there. He wanted to say, "Hey, McGee, Ol' Bean, I'm sorry. Come on, Bud, you're just as important to me as any old TV show. Let's go, let's do it together like we always do."

But Nicholas wouldn't.

He couldn't.

After all, he had his pride.

Finally, he stepped out into the hall and closed the door behind him.

The pad lay on the floor—lifeless and unmoving.

EIGHT
A Falling Star

The first thing Nicholas noticed was how drab and ordinary everything looked. After all, this was a TV studio! This was the home of Bill Banter and "Trash TV"! But as Nick and his family pulled into the parking lot, he thought the station looked just as dull and boring as any other building. No glitter, no spotlights, no names in lights. Just a dirty brick building with a few satellite dishes stuck on top.

That was the outside. The inside held even more disappointments.

First there was the receptionist. Like the building, she was bored and tired and seemingly lifeless. Nick couldn't understand. Didn't she know what an honor it was to be working there? Didn't she know how excited she should be? After all, she was rubbing shoulders with the stars!

He wanted to ask her about it, but he didn't have time. As soon as his dad told the woman who they were, she rose from the desk, telling them to follow her. She led them down a narrow, dimly lit hallway. Nick looked around. There, right there on the walls, so close that he could reach up and touch them, were photos of all sorts of grinning celebrities. Bob the weatherman, Julie Shimasaki the news anchorwoman, Sandy from "Afternoon at the Movies." They were all there! Nick could feel his heart begin to pound. This was it. This was *really* it.

With a grunt the receptionist pushed at the heavy door of the sound stage. There was a quiet *woosh* as it opened. They were hit with a wave of cold air from the air conditioning. That's not all they were hit with. They were also hit with color. Lots and lots of color. And light.

Nick sucked in his breath. Here they were. Right on the set of "Trash TV"! There were the Slime Slides to the left—*The* Slime Slides—the very ones he had seen so many times on TV! And over there, oh, over there was the scoreboard. There were the bleachers where the audience would boo and hiss and cheer and clap. Nick couldn't believe his eyes. He was really here.

"I don't give a rip about your budget! My contract calls for a hairdresser, and a hairdresser is what I expect!" The voice was shrill and loud and demanding. It was also strangely familiar. Nick squinted into the bright lights to see who it was.

"Bill, she's got the flu. Let somebody else take care of your hair, at least for today—"

"Shut up and get me that hairdresser! Do you hear me? I want that hairdresser and I want her now!"

It was Bill Banter! He stood not more than ten feet away! But this wasn't the Bill Banter Nick had seen on TV. This wasn't the good-looking, always-got-a-smile, wisecracking star everyone knew and loved. This guy was scrawny, skinny, and screaming.

"Bill—"

"Now!"

"Bill—"

"NOW!!"

"All right, all right. . . ." The other man moved off looking like a whipped puppy. Banter went back to studying his clipboard. Then he felt Nick's eyes on him and looked up.

Uh-oh, Nick thought. *I'm in for it now.*

But instead of screaming or throwing another temper tantrum, Banter suddenly broke into a grin. Not just any old grin. This one was so big you could see every one of his perfect, pearly whites.

Nicholas returned it nervously. He was a little confused. How could someone be such a creep one minute and such a nice guy the next? He didn't have long to think about it, though. Suddenly Banter crossed over to him and stuck out his hand for a shake. Nick took it. It was soft and cold and wet. "You must be Nicholas Martin. Glad to meet you."

"Hi" was about all Nick could say. Even that sounded more like a squeak than a word. It's not that he was a little nervous or anything like that. He was *a lot* nervous. This was Bill Banter. *Bill Banter, for crying out loud!*

Before Nick could say anything else—like tell Banter how excited he was or how funny and cool all his friends thought Banter was—the host turned and started shouting again. The smile on his face had disappeared as quickly as it had appeared. It was like he had some sort of "nice person" switch that could be turned off and on. Apparently he'd just found the off position again.

"WHERE'S THAT HAIRDRESSER? SYDNEY, YOU'VE GOT EXACTLY TEN SECONDS TO GET ME THAT HAIRDRESSER!"

"Places, everybody; we're on in five," a pleasant-looking man with headphones called out to the crew. Everyone began to run and make last-minute preparations.

Nick was up in the makeup chair. A lady was putting the final touches to his face. It was kind of embarrassing for a boy to get tan goop smeared all over his face. It was even more embarrassing smelling like your sister's makeup drawer. Still, if this was what a star had to put up with, then Nicholas knew he'd better get used to it.

He threw a glance over to the chair beside him. It was his opponent. The person he would be competing against on the show. Poor thing. It was pretty obvious she didn't stand a chance. Not against him.

For starters she was a *she*. Nick smiled smugly. Everyone knows boys are better at this sort of stuff than girls. Secondly, she was about as skinny and weak looking as they came. Now it's true, Nick wasn't the world's greatest jock. It was just that he was sure he'd have no problem beating this pathetic little creature. In fact, he could probably beat her with one arm tied behind his back. Or maybe two. Or maybe both arms and one foot. Or maybe . . . well, even if they tied whatever else *could* be tied back there, he knew he could still beat her.

In short, it was going to be a massacre.

Nick didn't mean to, but he couldn't help smiling. Today was going to be better than even he'd thought.

"Hello again, and welcome to 'TRASH TV!' "

The music blasted away. The kids in the audience clapped and cheered.

Nick tried to swallow, but his mouth was as dry as cotton. He stood backstage behind the set, waiting to go on. For a minute he thought about praying. Then he pushed the thought out of his head. He didn't need to pray. He'd made it this far on his own without bothering God. Why should he start now? Besides, he'd seen the girl he was competing against. Beating her would be a piece of cake.

He heard Bill Banter carrying on, being his usual, witty self. But from backstage, the man sounded hollow, kind of empty. Maybe it was because Nick had seen what he was really like— when he was screaming for a hairdresser. Or maybe it was because he had seen him without the makeup, the fancy clothes, and the adoring fans laughing at his every word.

As Nick waited, he reached out to touch the

back of the set. It was the same brightly colored set he had seen so many times on TV. But when he touched it, a piece broke off in his hand. He was startled. When he'd watched the show from home, everything had looked so sparkling, shiny, and expensive. Close up it was only styrofoam. Cheap, flimsy styrofoam. As for the sparkle and shine, it was just spray paint and regular ol' glitter—the type you could buy at any dime store.

Apparently, just like Bill Banter, nothing was as it appeared. Not when you got up close.

Banter was in his best form. "Our victims, er, contestants this week are . . . Amy Packer, from Ashcroft! Come on out, Amy!"

The kids cheered and clapped as Amy raced to her place beside Banter.

"And Nicholas Martin, from Eastfield!"

This was it! Nick took one last breath and ran out into the lights.

There was Banter grinning as big as ever. There were the cameras sending his picture across the universe. And there were the kids in the audience—all clapping and cheering for him. *Him.* Nicholas Martin, up-and-coming superstar.

"OK, my precious piggies," Banter teased. "You know the object of the game. Trash your opponent as often as possible and add up those points. The one with the highest score at the end of the game becomes our grand prize winner! So let's play . . . 'TRASH TV!' "

Before Nick knew it, an assistant swooped down and shoved a cowboy hat on his head. Then she tied a holster around his waist. Instead of guns, though,

it held squeeze bottles—one full of ketchup, the other full of mustard. Next, she shoved Nick to the center of the stage to face his opponent.

"OK, we're in the western mode here." Banter pointed to Nick. "You're Wyatt Burp." Then he pointed to little Amy. "You're Annie Oafly. You've got fifteen seconds to see who's the greatest food fighter in the West. Turn your backs to each other and at the count of three, draw."

Nicholas turned. This was going to be easier than he thought.

"One . . . Two . . . Three . . . DRAW!"

Nick spun around and began to squeeze the bottle. A direct hit! He got wimpy little Amy and he got her good!

"All right, trash her, TRASH HER!!" Banter rooted him on.

Nicholas went in for the kill. First the ketchup, then the mustard. Then the ketchup again. He was practically drowning the little girl. He completely covered her hair and face with the slimy goo.

Finally the buzzer went off and Nicholas raised his hands in victory. The audience went crazy—clapping and cheering and hooting. Nicholas had never felt such excitement in his life. He had never experienced such glory. Fortune and fame were his now! He could smell it. He could taste it. They were all his for the taking!

"All right!" Banter shouted over the cheers. "Nicholas wins that round with a big ten points!"

Nick kept on beaming, basking in the glory. He didn't bother to look over to Amy. She was history.

Had he bothered to look, he might not have been so sure of himself. Because he would have seen someone seething in anger. He would have seen someone setting her jaw, getting ready for revenge.

Now Nick and Amy stood behind two counters. A dozen pies were in front of each of them as Banter introduced the next competition.

"Now this ain't no piece of cake. In fact it's *Pie in the Eye*." The audience snickered. "Are you ready?"

The kids nodded.

"One, two . . . "

Nicholas was much more relaxed now. In fact, he even took a moment to look around. There was his family off to one side, grinning away. Well, why shouldn't they? He was doing them proud. Then there were the kids cheering him on. Why not? He was giving them a great show. Finally, there were those cameras—where Louis and Renee and Coach Slayter and Mr. Oliver and McGee and the whole world were watching . . . sharing in his victory.

" . . . three, THROW!"

For a second Nicholas hadn't heard Banter. The boy was so lost in his glory that he wasn't ready.

Amy, on the other hand, was.

She landed a banana cream pie smack dab in Nick's face. Before he could wipe his eyes to see what was going on she got him again . . . and again. One pie after another came flying in.

Nicholas began to cough and sputter. He liked banana cream, but not this much. If he could just get his goggles cleaned off . . . if he could just see where his pies were so he could grab them. Better yet, if he could just see where Amy was so he could dodge her pies. But he couldn't—and the pies just kept on coming.

At last the buzzer went off and it was over. But not really. Not by a long shot. The attack continued. . . .

Amy kept right on throwing—one pie after another after another. She was incredible. It was like she took out all of her anger from the last event and put it into throwing the pies. She wouldn't stop! She just kept right on throwing. Nicholas kept right on coughing and sputtering. It got to be so bad that Banter finally had to move in and start pulling her away.

"All right, all right," he laughed. "We have a real live one here, folks!"

At last Nicholas had a chance to wipe off the whipped cream and see what was going on. Then, when he saw what he saw, well . . . he wished he hadn't seen it. The audience was going crazy. They were clapping and laughing and shouting. Unfortunately, they weren't clapping and laughing and shouting for him. Not any more. Somehow they had started to side with Amy.

Weird, Nicholas thought. *You lose one little event and suddenly everyone turns on you.*

"That's OK," he muttered. "I'll show you. I'll show you all."

The next event was no better than the last.

It was a bean bag toss. Something anybody could do, right? After all, you just throw a bean bag through a hole in the wall. The only problem was the wall was halfway across the studio. Oh, and there was one other minor flaw . . . Amy was the star pitcher on her Little League team.

"All right! Amy gets another one! And another one! And another one! Come on, Nicholas, you're getting creamed!" (Banter never showed much sympathy for losers.)

As for the crowd—they were going nuts. They cheered and laughed and hissed. Only this time twice as loud. They were having the time of their lives watching this little twig, this little wimp of a girl massacring Nicholas. *Nicholas!* The Great Nicholas Martin.

Finally the buzzer sounded and the humiliation

was over. Well, not quite. The loser had a little reward coming. Suddenly, from high above, a huge bucket of flour dumped all over his head.

If the audience was having a good time before . . . well, they were rolling in the aisles now.

Once again Nick was coughing and choking— and covered with food. Only this time, instead of banana cream, he looked like a giant powdered doughnut. A very embarrassed and humiliated powdered doughnut.

Things were getting bad for Nicholas—very bad. What had once been a dream too good to be true was quickly turning into a nightmare. Still, it wasn't over yet. . . .

Now they were at the Slime Slides. Yes, *The* Slime Slides. Each slide was coated with thick, oozing chocolate. The idea was to climb up your slide, grab the flag at the top and slide back down. Simple. Except that you also had to balance a raw egg on a spoon which you held between your teeth. Oh, and if you slipped, there just happened to be a giant vat of chocolate waiting for you at the bottom.

Nick wasn't worried. He'd seen it done a zillion times. He could go up this slide in his sleep.

He crouched down at the bottom of the slide, waiting for the starting pistol. His muscles were tense, ready to leap into action. He'd had a couple of bad breaks before. That was all. He could make up for it now.

He stared at the flag . . . waiting.

Slowly, Banter raised the starting pistol.

The kids continued to cheer and jeer.

Nicholas paid no attention. He would win this one. True, he was behind in points. But if he put all his concentration into winning the Slime Slide, he could regain his lead, his dignity—and his pride.

He continued to stare . . . waiting . . . thinking . . . barely breathing.

Slowly Banter started to squeeze the trigger.

Nicholas continued to concentrate on the flag— his muscles taut, ready to thrust him into victory.

Finally the gun fired.

And they were off!

Well, at least Amy was. Nicholas had con- centrated so hard on the flag that he hadn't watched his feet. As he shoved off, his right foot slipped out from under him. He fell face first into the thick, gooey chocolate.

That was only the beginning.

Before he could catch himself, he landed belly- first on the slide . . . and he started to slide. He tried to grab the sides, but they were too slippery. It was only a couple of feet, but he couldn't stop. It was like a slow-motion nightmare. Then suddenly there was no slide under him. After a moment there was a tremendous *THWACK* as Nicholas did a perfect belly flop into the vat of chocolate. The sound echoed around the room as he slowly sank into the goop.

The studio audience screamed and roared with laughter.

"Oh no," Banter howled. "He's done it again!"

Nicholas wasn't giving up. He scampered back to his feet. Unfortunately he had no idea how slippery chocolate could be. Immediately his feet slid out from under him, and *SPLAT!* he landed back in the chocolate . . . rear first.

By now, the cameramen and crew were also laughing.

Again he tried and again his feet slipped out from under him. And again.

The audience howled so loud they sounded like a pack of wolves.

Finally Nicholas struggled back to his feet. By now he looked very much like a chocolate-covered peanut. He was totally covered with brown goop. In fact, if it hadn't been for the white of his eyes you wouldn't even have known which direction he was facing.

It didn't matter. Amy had made it to the top. She grabbed the flag and gracefully skated down the slide. There wasn't a spot of chocolate on her as she waved the flag to the cheering audience.

They began to chant, "A-MY! A-MY! A-MY!" It was worse than Nick could have ever imagined.

And so it went. Event after event after event. Fortunately, when he thought about it later, Nicholas couldn't remember everything. Only bits and pieces. Like the strawberry syrup poured over his hair. Or the pepper pile he fell into. (You'll never appreciate sneezing until you've fallen into a three-foot pepper pile.) Or the pillow fight.

Ah yes, the pillow fight. After the third or fourth hit, Amy's pillow exploded. Chicken feathers flew everywhere. Mostly they flew on Nick, who was still drenched in sticky chocolate. So wherever a feather landed, it stuck. Which meant they stuck everywhere!

In just a few minutes Nick had gone from Conquering Hero to Pie Face, to Powdered Doughnut, to Chocolate-Covered Peanut, to something the folks at Kentucky Fried Chicken might be eyeing. It was terrible.

All this *plus* the constant laughing, mocking, and finger pointing from his once-adoring audience.

Also, let's not forget those cameras. Those wonderful, friendly cameras that were catching the entire fiasco for the whole world to see. (When the cameramen weren't jiggling and bouncing them in laughter, that is.)

Basically, Nick wanted to disappear. He wanted to crawl into a hole and hide. But look as he might, there were no holes available.

How could this have happened? He had been so sure of himself. He *knew* he was better than this little girl. He knew he was better than just about anyone . . . his sisters, his friends, even McGee. After all *he* was the one who got on the show. *He* was the star. *He* was the one who was going to clean up on his helpless little opponent. So what in the world had happened?

Finally the last buzzer buzzed, and Nick was hustled off the set. Past the sarcastic Banter. Past the snickering cameramen. Past the shrieking audience.

At last he was out of the glaring lights of stardom.

But it was all there. It was all there in his

memory. The pain, the embarrassment, the humiliation. What had gone wrong?

It wasn't until the ride home that the answer started to come. Everyone was pretty quiet in the car. They didn't know what to say. That was OK. Nick probably wouldn't have heard them anyway. He just sat in the backseat, silent and aching, trying to hold back the tears.

Then, slowly, something started to come to his mind. Of all things, it was a Bible verse. *A Bible verse?* He didn't need a Bible verse. Not now. But it came to his mind and there was nothing he could do about it. It was a verse he had to memorize for Sunday school months ago. It didn't make a lot of sense to him then, so he never gave it much attention. It was just one of those verses you learn without ever knowing what it means. But for some reason it came back to him.

And for some reason it finally started to make sense. Not all at once, mind you. But by the time they finally got home, he began to understand:

"For everyone who tries to honor himself shall be humbled; and he who humbles himself shall be honored."

NINE
Reunion

I'd seen the whole thing on the tube. At first I was
kinda grinning when the little goof got clobbered.
Then it got worse and worse. Then, when you were
sure it couldn't get any worse, it got worse some
more.

Poor kid.

I mean, anyone who's ever waited too long to
throw a firecracker once it's lit knows that making
a mistake can be a painful thing. But making a mistake in front of the whole world can almost finish
you for good.

I guess that's how Nick must have felt. He must
have figured everything was ruined. No fans. No
fame. And, what's worse, no friends.

That's where he was wrong.

These last few days it seemed like our whole
world had turned upside down. Sometimes that
kind of thing shakes you loose from the people you
care most about. If you stop to think about it,
though, you'd find that nothing's more important

than those people—'cause they're the ones who never stop caring and believing in you.

After seeing him get slaughtered on TV, I knew Nick needed to know that. I also knew I needed to tell him. Finally I heard the car drive up, and I heard him clumping up the stairs to his room. At last he threw open the door. The kid looked beat. I mean, he gave a whole new definition to the word whipped.

He didn't see me and he didn't say a word. He just dragged himself over to the bed and collapsed. Poor guy.

I quietly crossed to the bed and climbed up onto the pillow. Nick's eyes were clenched tight. Even at that a tear managed to sneak out and slowly move

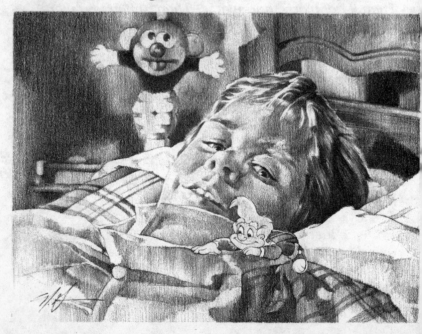

across his cheek. I eased down on the pillow beside him and gently leaned my back against his
shoulder.

After a minute he opened his eyes.

I gave him my best "You-OK-Little-Buddy?" look.
Then I reached out and gently patted him on the
shoulder. And he did what any best buddy in the
whole wide world would do—he smiled.

We were gonna make it. We were gonna regroup,
learn from our mistake, and probably take more
lumps along the way.

But we were gonna do it together.

TEN
Wrapping Up

Monday was crummy.

The week before, Nicholas had hoped everyone would watch the show. Unfortunately his wish had come true. Now it seemed like everyone had something to say.

"Nice work, champ . . . or should I say 'chump'?"

"You stunk so bad I could smell it over my TV."

"Look out! It's the human Hershey bar!"

Of course he pretended to laugh and smile along with them. Inside, though, whatever was left of his pride just kept on dying.

Even Heather treated him differently. Oh, she still threw him an occasional glance from time to time. But the way her eyes crinkled and the way she covered her mouth as she leaned over to talk to her friends . . . well, it was pretty obvious she was laughing. She wasn't laughing *with* Nicholas, though. She was laughing *at* him.

Finally the three o'clock bell rang. At last Nicholas could head for home. He moved out the front doors and down the steps. It was raining.

Somehow that didn't surprise him.

"Hey, Mr. Big Shot! What happened?" It was Louis. Well, at least here was somebody who would understand—someone who would still be his buddy.

"So where's all your friends now?" he smirked. Before Nicholas could answer, Louis turned and headed off, snickering all the way.

Nick took a deep breath and let it out. He couldn't blame Louis. He knew he'd been a jerk. In fact, he'd been a certifiable, cream-of-the-crop creep. Whatever his friends dished out over the next few days he probably deserved. He knew it wouldn't last forever—but he also knew it wasn't going to be a lot of fun.

"Not a great day, huh?" It was Jamie.

Nick couldn't help but grin. It was nice to finally see a friendly face.

"Sure you want to hang out with the all-school idiot?" he asked.

"That's OK, I'm used to it."

He wasn't sure if that was a compliment or not. Still, he knew she meant well. Even though everyone else had turned their back on him, Jamie was still there. His little sister. True to the end.

"So tell me," Nicholas asked, "how's that wombat of yours coming?"

Jamie grimaced. "It's due tomorrow. Jenny Michelson says it looks like a porcupine from Mars."

Nicholas tried to swallow back his laughter. "Well, maybe I can give you a hand with it."

"Hey guys . . ."

They looked up. It was Mom. She was standing, waiting in the rain.

"Mom, what are you doing here?" Nicholas asked in surprise.

"I've been answering phones at the counseling center."

They joined her and headed for the car.

"You mean you took the job?" Nicholas asked. With the show and all he'd almost forgotten about the decision Mom had had to make about the counseling center job.

"Yup," she said as she smiled at Nicholas. "I'm afraid you're not the only one getting to learn humility."

Nicholas grinned. "So that's what I've been learning."

She reached over and put her arm around him. "That's what we've *both* been learning, kiddo."

"Not a lot of fun, is it?" Nicholas teased.

Mom grinned back knowingly. "It's something we all need," she said with a sigh.

They arrived at the car, and she opened the door for them to climb in. "God gives strength to the humble," she quoted. "But flattens the hotshots."

Nicholas had to laugh as he crawled into the car.

"Truer words were never spoken," I said to myself as Nicholas and I settled into the backseat. However, it seemed to me that they could be spoken a bit more poetically. So I lifted up the cover to my scratch pad and added. "Sure, it's like I always say, 'If you think you're a hotshot, watch out for

game shows with chock-o-lot!'"

"McGee," Nick groaned. *The kid never did have a great sense of humor.* Then he shot me a sly smile. "How 'bout: 'If you keep making jokes so bad, watch out for slamming sketch pads!' "

Boy, his rhymes were worse than mine.

"Uh, no . . . ," I gently corrected. "Oh, here we go: 'If you're a kid that's stuck-up, plan to get mustarded and ketch-uped.' "

The last thing I saw was the curl of Nicholas's lip just before he brought the sketch pad cover down on top of me! I made a last ditch effort to reason with him. "Hey, wait a min—"

Slam! went the pad.

If you've ever tried talking with your jaws wired shut or with a mouth full of biscuits, you can understand why I suddenly sounded like this:

"Mikomas! . . . Met me out of mere . . . MIKOMUS!"

The worst part about trying to talk with your mouth closed is that you can still hear what other people say.

"Did you say something?" Mrs. Mom asked as she climbed into the other side of the car.

"It's nothing, Mom," Nick replied.

Nothing! Why that little sneak! "MIKOMUS! OPEN MISS MAD!" *I shouted. It was no use. His bony little hand just held the cover down more firmly.*

"Nothing at all," he chuckled, *and I could tell he was smiling.*

OK, kid. You just keep it up, I thought. Enjoy yourself while you can. I already know about the next chapter in our little adventures. And believe me, Buddy Boy, it makes this last episode look like a picnic . . . with ants . . . (and maybe even a few uncles)!